Boris and the Blueberry Adventure

For Kosma, Abraham and Eliasz

"Children see magic because they look for it."

Christopher Moore

Boris and the Blueberry Adventure

Text and illustrations copyright © 2020 by Dorota Lagida-Ostling

Published 2020 by Psokot Books
Printed in the United States of America
ISBN: 978-1-7353312-1-8

Boris and the Blueberry Adventure

By Dorota Lagida-Ostling

Boris came from the city to stay with his Grandma for a while.
"Boris, take this little pail and bring me some elderberries,"
said Grandma.
"I'd like to make cough syrup.
Elderberries are the best for cough syrup".

Boris took the pail and went straight into the woods.

He knew about blueberries,
and blackberries,
and strawberries,
and raspberries,
but he had never heard of elder berries.

"I know what elder means," he thought.
"It just means older.
I hope I know them when I see them."

As he walked he peeked inside the yellow pail.
Grandma must have slipped something special into it,
because he smiled and hopped a little.

He started his search
right away.

He looked thoroughly among bushes
and under leaves.

He looked left and right,
and up and down.

But what he saw was just...
...blueberries.

And none of them were older than the others.

And then,
he saw something big and blue in the clearing.
It looked like it had fallen from the sky.

Boris approached it with caution.
He touched it, put his cheek next to it, and smelt it.

What a surprise!

A bed in the middle of the forest!

He tossed a little and made himself comfortable.

But as soon as he
fell asleep, his bed woke up.

And it wasn't a bed
anymore...

It was

The Giant Blue Bear!

And he was HUNGRY!!!

The Giant Blue Bear looked around.

Something yellow was nesting in his fur.

Someone small was sleeeping on top of him.

And he couldn't wait to eat.

But he didn't want to wake up the sleeping person…

…and promptly set to work picking his favorite blueberries.

But while he was reaching for one very juicy berry...

...Boris woke up!

Luckily, The Giant Blue Bear was very polite.

"I am Boris,"
Boris introduced himself
properly.

"Who are you?"

"I'm
The Giant Blue Bear
of course,"
said the bear.
"You may call me Blue.
Do you want to play?"

They played catch-a-berry

until all the berries were gone.

"What would you like to do now?" asked Blue.

"I have to find elder berries for Grandma," said Boris.
"I looked and looked and looked, but none of the berries
were older than the others."

"Elderberries aren't just older blueberries,"
Blue chuckled. "They're a completely different fruit!

And they don't grow in the forest. I'll show you!"

When they reached the edge of the woods, Blue said,

"Look at that little white house.
Can you see the shrubs?
The best elderberries grow there."

"But it's Grandma's house!" said Boris.
"I didn't have to go into the forest at all!"

But I'm so glad you did, Boris,

because

unplanned

things

often

work out

BEST!

I feel like I've known you

for a really long time...

And I'm glad too, Blue!

But now I must go,
Goodbye Blue...

Goodbye, Boris.
Let's play again soon!

Boris was happy to see Grandma
waiting for him.

"Grandma...
...I didn't bring
the elderberries,"
said Boris.

"That's all right, Boris,
we'll pick them together,"
said Grandma.

"And Grandma...
thank you
for putting Blue
into the pail.
We had so much fun!"

"You're welcome, darling.
I noticed you forgot him."

CPSIA information can be obtained
at www.ICGtesting.com
Printed in the USA
LVHW071957220920
666819LV00031B/867